O9-AIG-850

Dear Parents:

Congratulations! Your child is taking the first steps on an exciting journey. The destination? Independent reading!

STEP INTO READING® will help your child get there. The program offers five steps to reading success. Each step includes fun stories and colorful art or photographs. In addition to original fiction and books with favorite characters, there are Step into Reading Non-Fiction Readers, Phonics Readers and Boxed Sets, Sticker Readers, and Comic Readers—a complete literacy program with something to interest every child.

Learning to Read, Step by Step!

Ready to Read   Preschool–Kindergarten
• big type and easy words • rhyme and rhythm • picture clues
For children who know the alphabet and are eager to begin reading.

Reading with Help   Preschool–Grade 1
• basic vocabulary • short sentences • simple stories
For children who recognize familiar words and sound out new words with help.

Reading on Your Own   Grades 1–3
• engaging characters • easy-to-follow plots • popular topics
For children who are ready to read on their own.

Reading Paragraphs   Grades 2–3
• challenging vocabulary • short paragraphs • exciting stories
For newly independent readers who read simple sentences with confidence.

Ready for Chapters   Grades 2–4
• chapters • longer paragraphs • full-color art
For children who want to take the plunge into chapter books but still like colorful pictures.

STEP INTO READING® is designed to give every child a successful reading experience. The grade levels are only guides; children will progress through the steps at their own speed, developing confidence in their reading.

Remember, a lifetime love of reading starts with a single step!

Materials and characters from the movie *Cars*. Copyright © 2014 Disney•Pixar. Disney•Pixar elements © Disney•Pixar, not including underlying vehicles owned by third parties; and, if applicable: Model T is a trademark of Ford Motor Company; Corvette is a trademark of General Motors; and Mazda Miata is a trademark of Mazda Motor Corporation. Published in the United States by Random House Children's Books, a division of Random House LLC, 1745 Broadway, New York, NY 10019, and in Canada by Random House of Canada Limited, Toronto, Penguin Random House Companies, in conjunction with Disney Enterprises, Inc.

Step into Reading, Random House, and the Random House colophon are registered trademarks of Random House LLC.

Visit us on the Web!
StepIntoReading.com
randomhouse.com/kids

Educators and librarians, for a variety of teaching tools, visit us at randomhouse.com/teachers

ISBN 978-0-7364-3217-7 (trade) — ISBN 978-0-7364-8151-9 (lib. bdg.) — ISBN 978-0-7364-3218-4 (ebook)

Printed in the United States of America   10 9 8 7 6 5 4 3 2 1

DISNEY · PIXAR

Cars

RACING FOR GOOD

Adapted by Ruth Homberg

Based on the original story by Annie Auerbach

Illustrated by the Disney Storybook Art Team

Random House 🏠 New York

Lightning McQueen

is a race car.

Jeff Gorvette is
a race car, too.
They are good friends.

Lightning and Jeff
have an idea.

They will have
a special race.
They will raise money
to help old cars.
It is a race for good.

Race day is here!

Chick Hicks comes.

Lots of cars are excited

to race.

Chick does not want
to race for good.
He wants to win money.

Chick thinks he is
the fastest racer.
He wants to win
no matter what.

The cars line up.
Lightning and Francesco
are ready.

They wish
each other luck.

Ready, set, go!

The race starts.

The cars zoom
around the track.
Racing is fun!
Who will win?

The cars go fast.

The crowd cheers.

Francesco is
in first place.
Lightning is
in second place!

Chick zooms ahead.

He passes Nigel.

Bash!

Chick bashes cars
out of his way.

Chick rams Francesco.

Francesco swerves.

Crash!

Chick hits the wall.

Can he still win?

Jeff and Lightning wink
at each other.
They let Chick pass them.
He crosses
the finish line.

Chick wins the race!
He cannot wait
to get his prize.

CHICK
HICKS

Chick drives

onto the stage.

He will not keep
the prize money.
Jeff and Lightning
will use it
to help older cars.

Lightning and Jeff
thank Chick for
racing for good.

Chick is mad.

He wants to keep

the prize money!

Francesco cheers.

He did not win.

But he likes to

help others.

Lizzie thanks Chick.
His prize money
will help her friends.

Chick speeds away.

Lightning and Jeff
are happy
they helped others.

A race for good
is the best kind
of race.

Everyone wins!